D0515759

Howdy!

My name is Denni-Jo and
I'm a real-life cowgirl. I ride horses
and rope cattle on our ranch. We have horses,
cows, dogs, and cats—which means plenty of chores.
It doesn't matter if you are a boy or girl, big or small;
everyone pitches in and does their share. Once the
chores are done there's plenty of time for fun—
and surprises! Join me, and my
pony, Pinto, on an adventure
neither of us will soon forget.
Saddle up and let's go!

www.denni-jo.com

Text © 2017 by Buck Buchanan
Illustrations ©2017 by Christina Wald

All right reserved. No part of this book may be reproduced or
transmitted in any form or by any means, electronic or mechanical,
including photocopying, recording, or by any information storage
system, without written permission of the publisher.

Library of Congress Cataloging-in-Publication Data

Names: Buchanan, Buck, 1955- author. | Wald, Christina, illustrator.
Title: Denni-Jo and Navajo / by Buck Buchanan ; illustrated by
    Christina Wald.
Description: Portland, Oregon : WestWinds Press, [2017] |
    Summary: A seven-year-old ranch girl gets permission from her
    mom to ride her pony Navajo solo across the ranch to visit her
    grandparents and has exciting experiences along the way.
Identifiers: LCCN 2015034602 | ISBN 9781943328468 (hardcover)
Subjects: | CYAC: Ranch life—Fiction.
Classification: LCC PZ7.1.B815 De 2017 | DDC [E]—dc23 LC record
    available at https://lccn.loc.gov/2015034602

Editor: Michelle McCann

Designed and produced with care by Jane Freeburg
Collaborative Publishing Services, Bozeman, Montana

WestWinds Press® an imprint of

GRAPHIC ARTS
BOOKS®

www.graphicartsbooks.com

Printed in China

Denni-Jo
and Pinto

Bridger Public Library

Buck Buchanan
ILLUSTRATED BY CHRISTINA WALD

Denni-Jo woke up and looked out her window. The late spring sun lit up the sagebrush-covered hills and the green willows that hugged the banks of the creek.

Time to get up!

She slipped on her jeans, her favorite shirt, and her boots and hat. Denni-Jo thought, *This is the perfect day for adventure!*

Denni-Jo bounded into the kitchen following the delicious smell of bacon.

"Good morning!" she called out. "Today is the perfect day for adventure!"

"Do you have something in mind?" asked her mother.

"Can I ride Pinto to Granny P and Papa D's ranch by myself?" she asked. "It's only two miles away."

"Well, you *have* ridden there with your dad and me. But you *are* only seven. . . ."

"Almost eight!" interrupted Denni-Jo.

"In *nine months* you will be eight," said her mother. Then she smiled. "Okay, Denni-Jo, you can go by yourself. But you have to be careful. I'll call your grandparents and let them know."

"Hooray!" whooped Denni-Jo. "It's great being almost eight!"

After she finished breakfast and her chores, Denni-Jo raced to the corral, where her paint pony was waiting for her.

"Guess what, Pinto?" she asked, rubbing his forehead. "Today we're going on an adventure!"

Pinto pricked up his ears and nickered. Denni-Jo shook a pan of oats and he moved his head up and down. Pinto loved oats.

As Pinto ate breakfast, Denni-Jo slipped a halter over his head. Once she saddled and bridled her pony, she packed her saddlebags: hay pellets for Pinto in one; a water canteen and a book for herself in the other. Denni-Jo never went anywhere without a book.

"Ready!" She patted Pinto with satisfaction.

Denni-Jo swung up into the saddle and waved. "Granny P and Papa D are expecting you for lunch," called her mother. "Go straight there!"

"Yes, ma'am," said Denni-Jo, giving her a salute.

Pulling her hat down tight, she prodded Pinto with the heels of her boots and they trotted off along the cow trail leading to her grandparents' ranch.

Denni-Jo relaxed and took a good look around. The sweet smell of sagebrush tickled her nose. Hazy purple mountains surrounded the high desert ranch lands. A ribbon of green marked the distant stream, and a hawk called out far up in the sky.

Whirrr! Whiiiirrrr! Off to Denni-Jo's right the unmistakable buzz of a rattlesnake shattered the still air. Pinto did not flinch.

"Easy, boy!" said Denni-Jo. "That rattler is just hunting mice and ground squirrels, not cowgirls and ponies."

Pinto sidestepped, then continued on his way.

"What a good pony not to shy from that old snake," said Denni-Jo.

With the danger behind her, the sun steady on her hat, and the rhythmic *clomp-clomp-clomp-clomp* of Pinto's hooves, Denni-Jo began to drift off, just like when her mother read her a bedtime story.

Out of nowhere a jackrabbit bolted across the trail. Right in front of Pinto! Startled, Pinto reared up on his hind legs.

Denni-Jo launched out of the saddle like a rocket! Her boot hooked the saddle horn, and she bounced against Pinto's side as he galloped straight up the hillside.

With her free hand Denni-Jo grabbed Pinto's mane. Using all of her strength, she hoisted herself back up into the saddle.

"Whoa boy, WHOA!" yelled Denni-Jo, as she hauled back on the reins. Pinto slowed to a stop beside the creek. "Wow, that was close," Denni-Jo whispered to Pinto, rubbing his neck.

"My boot saved me. Guess they're my lucky boots now!" she said with a laugh. Denni-Jo straightened her hat.

Suddenly something upstream caught her eye. It was a big red and white cow with her family's brand on its left ribs.

"What's she doing here?" wondered Denni-Jo. "We moved our cattle out of this pasture two days ago. She must be lost."

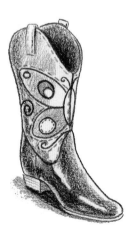

Denni-Jo and Pinto set out to investigate. As they got closer, they could see why the cow was there—her calf was stuck in a muddy bog by the creek.

Momma Cow was staying nearby to protect her baby, but she had no idea how to get it out of the sticky mud.

"If we don't get that calf out of there, it will die!" said Denni-Jo.

"But Momma Cow won't want us near her baby. A mad momma cow is nothing to mess with! We've got to distract her. Got any ideas?" she asked Pinto, who flicked his ears in response.

Denni-Jo took off her hat and scratched her head. "I know! The hay pellets!" she said. "Sorry, Pinto, but if I drop them away from the calf, maybe Momma Cow will go eat them. While she's busy we can rope the calf and pull it out."

They skirted the edge of the bog and rode as close to Momma Cow as they dared.

"Steady, Pinto," whispered Denni-Jo as she unbuckled a saddlebag and grabbed a handful of hay pellets. She slid down and set the pellets in a pile. After swinging back into the saddle, Denni-Jo squeezed her legs and Pinto moved away from the cow.

Soon Momma Cow smelled the hay pellets and sauntered over to taste them.

Now's our chance," said Denni-Jo. She unfastened her lariat and built a loop. She twirled the rope over her head a few times, then let the looped end fly.

"Shucks, I missed!" Quickly, she built another loop and threw again. This time the calf ducked out of the rope.

"NUTS!" said Denni-Jo.

The calf let out a loud cry: MAA-AAH! Momma Cow twirled around to see what was tormenting her baby.

Uh-oh," said Denni-Jo. "I've got one more try."
Denni-Jo had never built a loop so fast!
She threw without thinking. The loop settled over the
calf's head, this time low enough so it couldn't slip out.
"Perfect shot!" she hollered.
She took a few dallies around her saddle horn, then
turned Pinto downstream. The rope tightened and the calf
struggled, but still didn't come out of the muck.

Here comes Momma Cow," muttered Denni-Jo, "and boy, is she
mad. Hurry up and pull, Pinto. PULL!"

"You can do it!" cried Denni-Jo. Pinto strained against the rope.
The calf thrashed in the mud. Suddenly, with a giant
SHUUH-LLUK the calf was free!

With the tired, muddy calf in tow and Momma Cow bringing up the rear, Denni-Jo and Pinto trotted up and over the next hill. She could see her grandparents' ranch down in the bottom of the draw.

As she neared the ranch, Denni-Jo yelled,
"Open the gate! OPEN THE GATE! OPEN THE GATE!"
    Granny P pulled open the gate and in trotted Denni-Jo on Pinto,
her pigtails bouncing, leading their missing stock.

What a sight," said Granny P, "it's a three-critter parade!"

"What have you been up to, Denni-Jo?" asked Papa D.

"We found the calf stuck in the mud, so we got it unstuck," she answered. She didn't tell the rest of her story— the rattlesnake and the rabbit. That could happen later.

"You were supposed to come straight here, young lady," chuckled Granny P. "But nice work saving that calf, cowgirl."

During lunch, Denni-Jo told them the whole adventure over seconds of everything, plus a slice of Granny P's delicious apple pie.

"Well, well," said Papa D, "that's mighty fine work for a buckaroo who's only seven."

"For crying out loud!" exclaimed Denni-Jo, a smile creeping across her face as wide as the brim of her hat. "I'm almost eight!"

Glossary

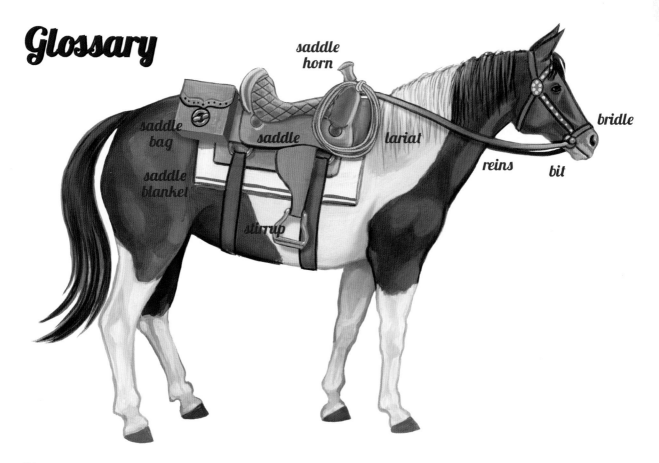

saddle horn

saddle bag

saddle

saddle blanket

stirrup

lariat

bridle

reins

bit

Bit The metal mouthpiece attached to the bridle and reins, it sends a cowgirl's message to her horse.

Brand A permanent mark on an animal's hide to show livestock ownership.

Bridle The leather and metal headgear used to communicate with a horse.

Buckaroo A person who really understands horses and cattle.

Dally, dallies Windings of the lariat around the saddle horn.

Hay pellets Compressed hay and/or grain.

Lariat The stiff braided rope used to work cattle or horses.

Paint A breed of horse with white and dark color patterns on its hide; also called a pinto.

Pony A small horse, or an affectionate term for a favorite horse.

Reins Long pieces of leather or rope that attach to the bit on the bridle and help a cowgirl give signals to her horse.

Rope, roping To capture a cow, calf, or horse with a lariat.

Saddle A leather seat that allows buckaroos to ride a horse with safety and control.

Saddle blanket A pad placed between the horse and the saddle.

Shy A startled movement a horse makes when alarmed.

Stirrup A foot loop where a cowgirl puts her boot to mount, dismount, and remain in the saddle.

Stock Short for livestock; animals on a ranch.

Tack A horse's gear—halter, bridle, saddle, saddle blanket, saddlebags, etc.